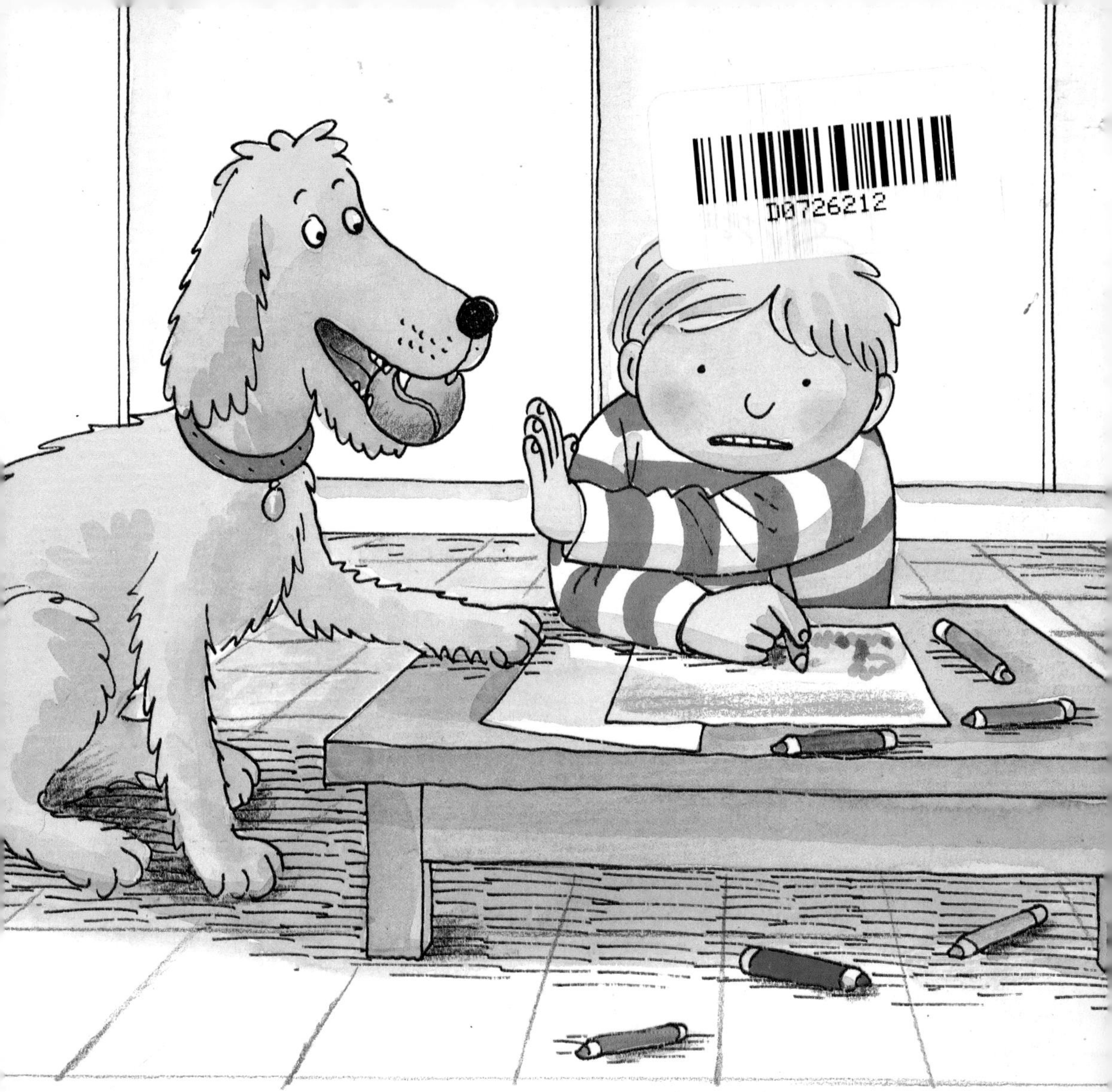

Go away, Floppy.

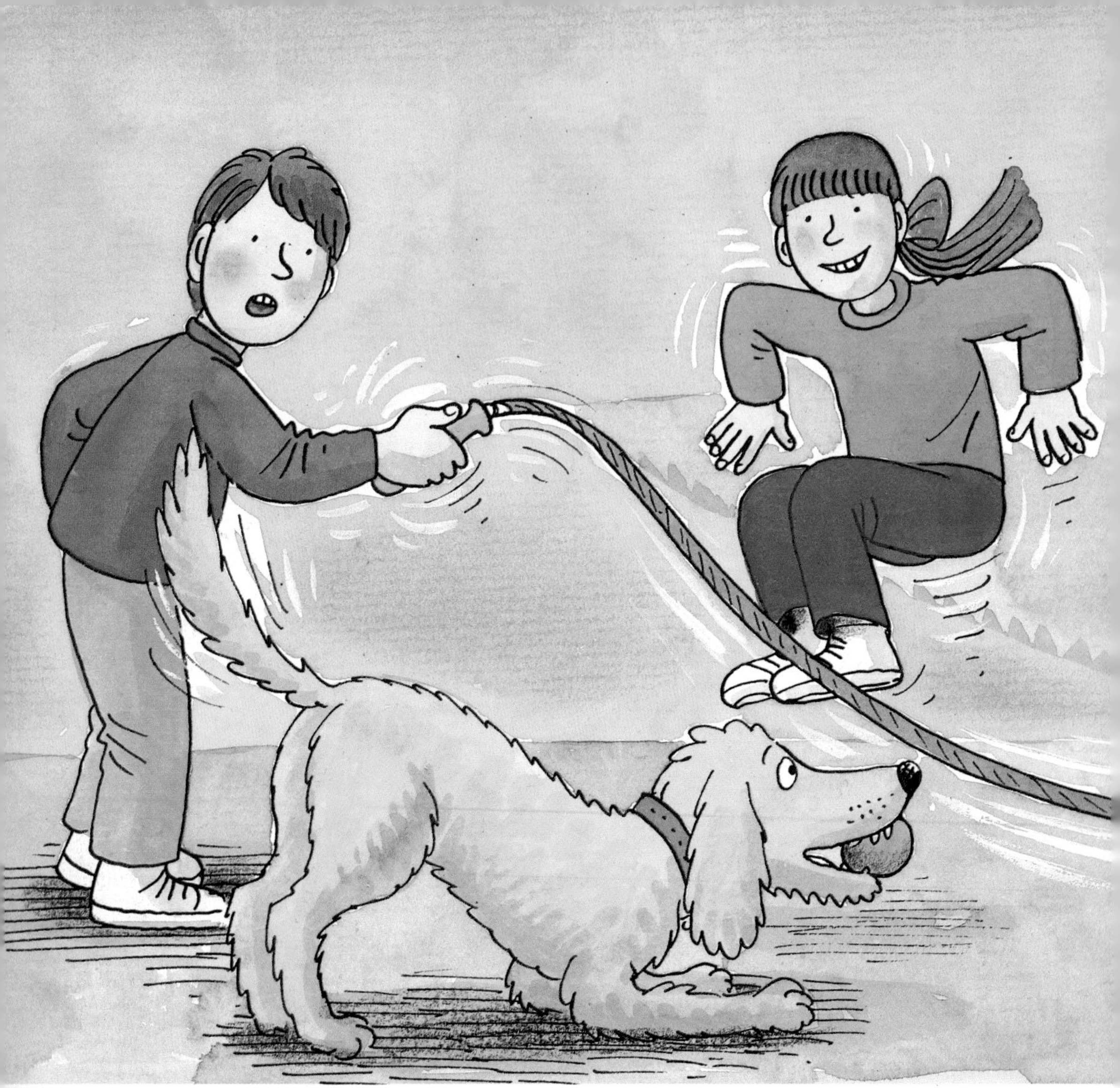

Go away, Floppy.

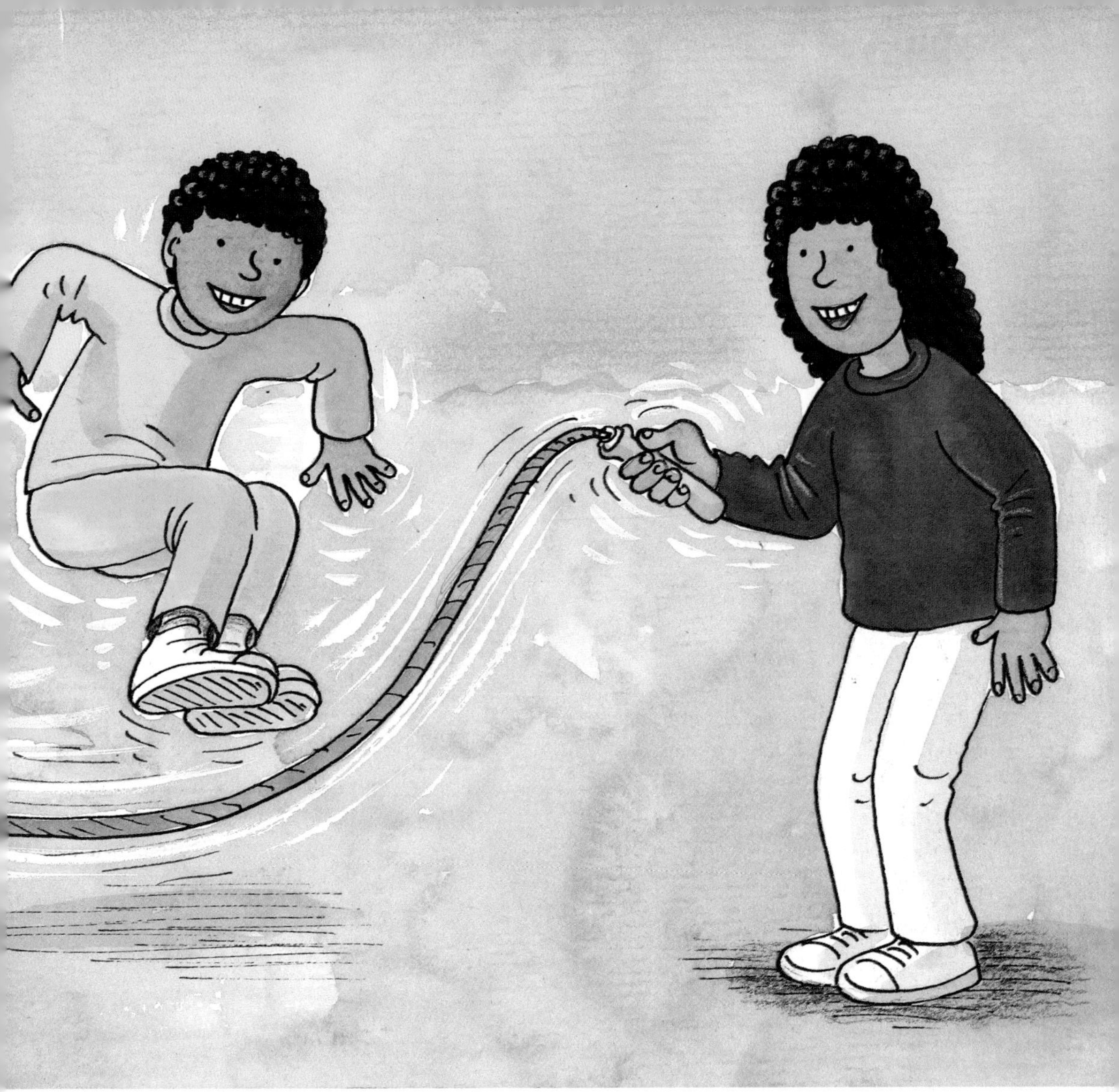

We are skipping.

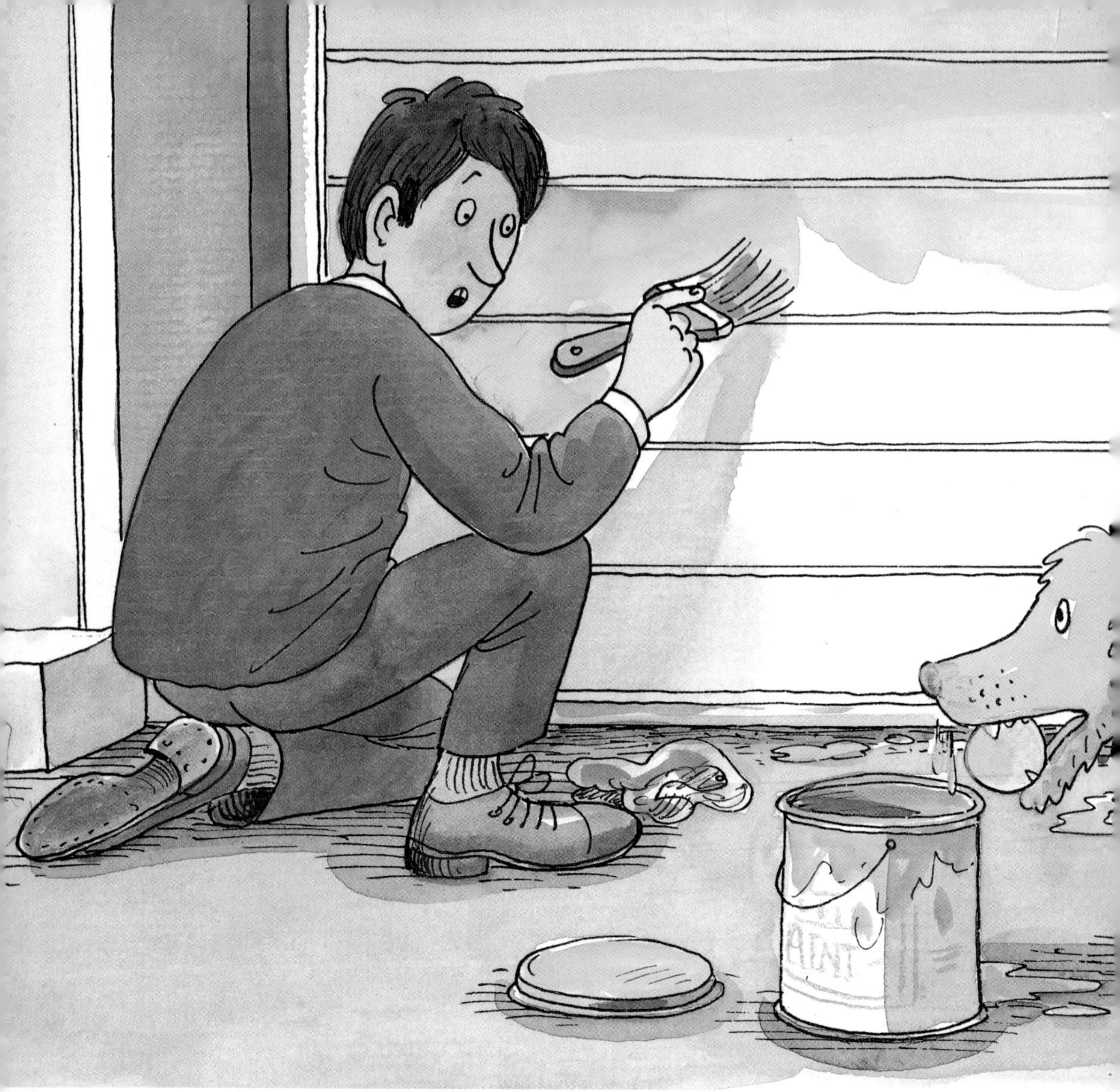

Go away, Floppy.

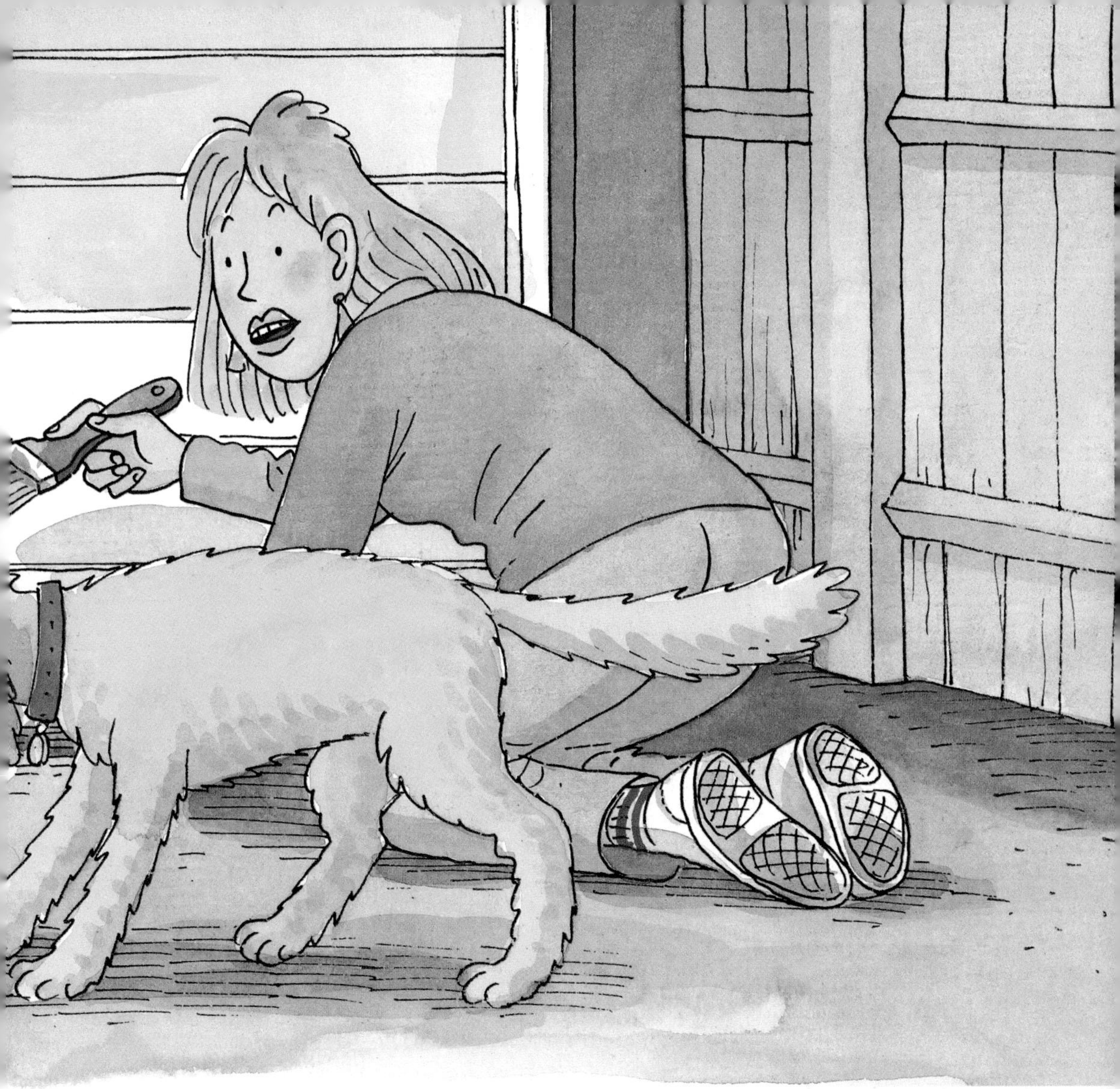

We are painting.

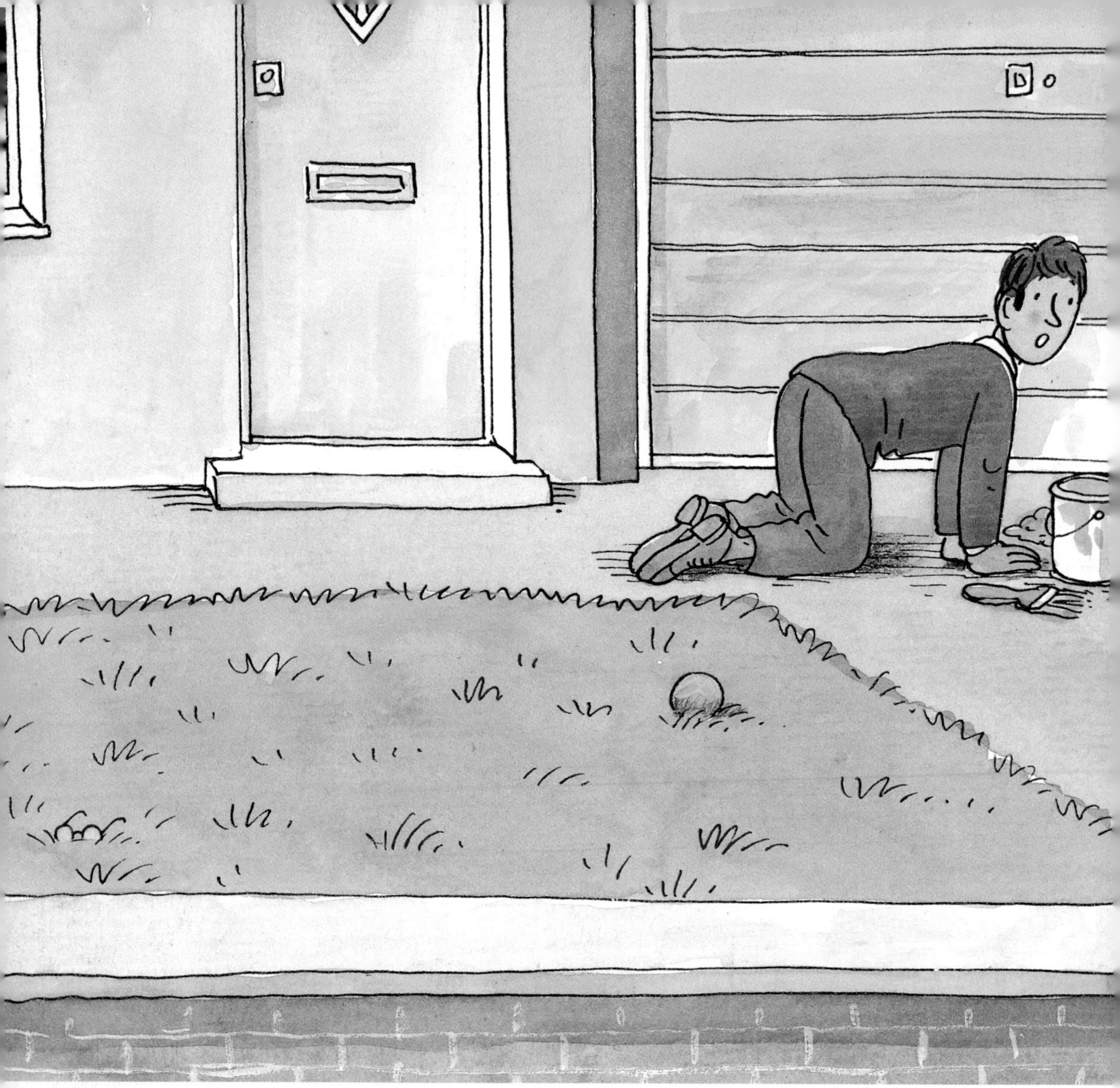

Come back, Floppy.

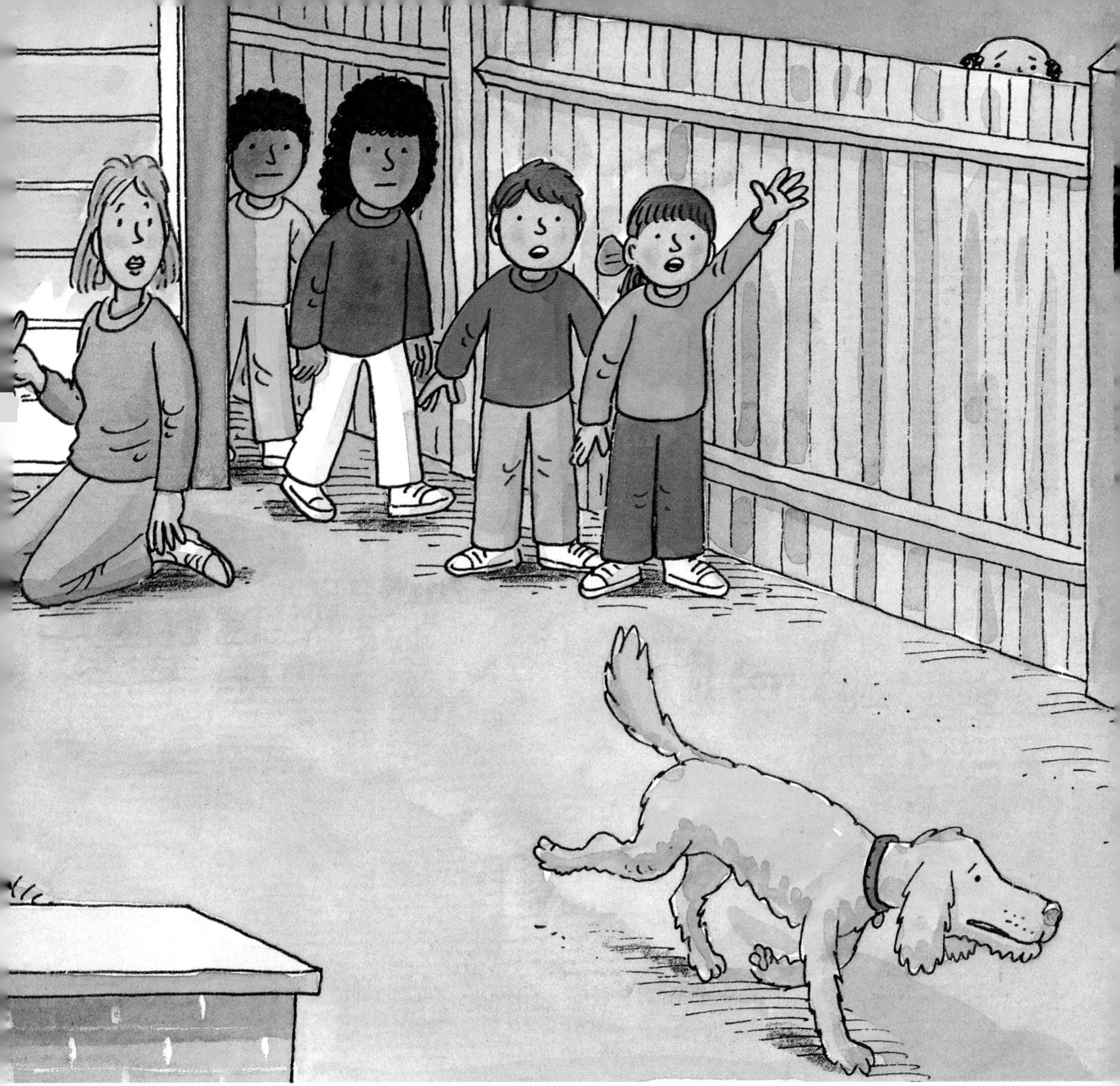

Floppy, come back.

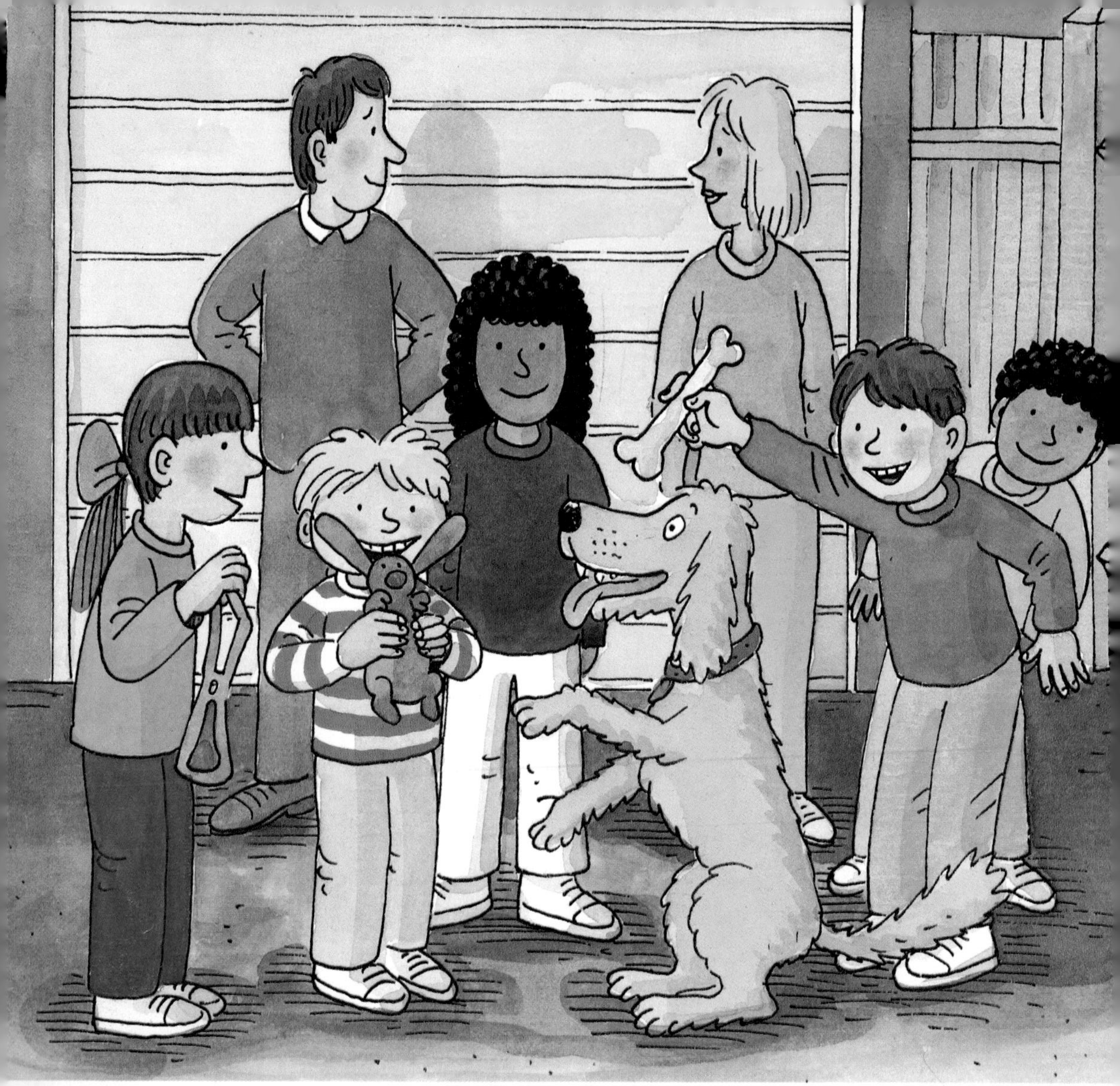

We are sorry.

Printed in Hong Kong